THE BIG RACE

DAVID BARROW

Hodder

The Big Race was very tough.

Only the **fastest**, **biggest** and **strongest** animals could take part.

"I'd like to enter please," said little Aardvark.

"What? You?" said Lion. "You'll never finish."

"Oh, yes I will!" said Aardvark.

Cheetah was very **fast**.
Buffalo was very **big**.
And Crocodile was
very **strong**.

"You'll never finish!"
they sniggered.

"I will, and
I'll have fun,"
said Aardvark.

The animals lined up
at the start. It was
going to be the race
of their lives.

Warthog
called out:

"On your
marks ...

get set ...

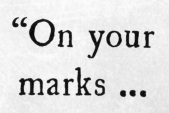

... **go!**" They charged across the dusty desert.

Cheetah was in the **lead** ...

Buffalo was close **behind** ...

and Crocodile too!

Aardvark was hot on their heels.

They cycled up the hill.

Buffalo pushed into **first** place ...

Crocodile puffed into **second** place ...

and Cheetah slipped into **third** place.

Aardvark was close behind.

They plunged down the waterfall.

Buffalo did
backstroke ...

Cheetah did a
cannonball ...

and Crocodile dived
in **head first.**

"Whee!!" laughed Aardvark.

The animals swam **under** the water ...

and wobbled **over** the valley.

Aardvark was very tired.

But she'd never give up.

The others **powered** onwards
through the woods ...

and upwards into the air.

The Big Race was
almost over.

"Maybe the other
animals were right."
sighed Aardvark.
Perhaps I'll never finish."

Then all of a sudden ...

Aardvark tumbled down
through the air ...

past Buffalo ...

past Cheetah ...

past Crocodile ...

NISH

and landed safely almost
at the finish line.

But the others were
coming up behind her ...

Would Aardvark make it?

WHOOSH!

Cheetah, Buffalo and Crocodile couldn't agree on who had crossed the finish line first.

But Aardvark had shown everyone that you don't need to be the fastest, biggest or strongest to join in and have fun.

She **did finish** the Big Race.
And she got a medal.

"**Hooray** for Aardvark," all her friends cheered.

For Martin and Pam. This is all their fault.

Big thanks to Sam.

HODDER CHILDREN'S BOOKS

First published in Great Britain in 2018 by Hodder and Stoughton

Text and illustration copyright © David Barrow, 2018

The moral rights of the author and illustrator have been asserted.

All rights reserved

A CIP catalogue record for this book is available from the British Library.

HB ISBN: 978 1 444 92928 7

PB ISBN: 978 1 444 92929 4

1 3 5 7 9 10 8 6 4 2

Printed and bound in China

Hodder Children's Books, an imprint of Hachette Children's Group,
part of Hodder and Stoughton

Carmelite House, 50 Victoria Embankment, London, EC4Y 0DZ

An Hachette UK Company
www.hachette.co.uk

www.hachettechildrens.co.uk